Ziggy's Big Adventure

For Poppy Smailes,
and Bumble and Bee the kittens,
with lots of love – SM

STRIPES PUBLISHING
An imprint of Magi Publications
1 The Coda Centre, 189 Munster Road,
London SW6 6AW

A paperback original
First published in Great Britain in 2010

Text copyright © Sue Mongredien, 2010
Illustrations copyright © Artful Doodlers, 2010
Photographs copyright © iStockphoto.com, 2010

ISBN: 978-1-84715-141-4

A CIP catalogue record for this book is available
from the British Library.

Printed and bound in the UK.

10 9 8 7 6 5 4 3 2 1

Sue Mongredien

Kitten Club

Ziggy's Big Adventure

Stripes

Meet the Kitten Club girls!

Amy
& Ginger

Mia
& Smokey

Molly
& Truffle

Ella
& Honey

Ruby
& Ziggy

Lily
& Buster

Chapter I

Ruby Jackson peered out of the car window at the houses. "Twenty-four ... twenty-six ... twenty-eight," she said. "That's it, there, Mum – number twenty-eight; the one with the red door."

As her mum parked at the side of the road, Ruby turned to grin at her two friends, Molly and Lily, who were sitting on the

back seat. It was Saturday afternoon, which meant only one thing: Kitten Club! This week they were meeting at Ella's house.

"Have fun," said Ruby's mum, as the girls unclipped their seat belts. "I'll pick you up at five. Oh, and Ruby, don't forget to invite everyone to the You-Know-What."

Ruby grinned. "I won't," she said. "See you later."

Ruby got out of the car and opened the back door for Lily and Molly. The door had a child lock on as Ruby's little brother, Max, was only four, and a bit of a handful! He was at home with Dad now, thank goodness.

"What's the You-Know-What?" Molly asked, climbing out. "Ooh – is it something to do with your birthday next week?"

Ruby pretended to zip up her lips. She and Molly were best friends and usually told each other *everything*, but Ruby wanted this to be a secret for a little while longer. "Wait and see," was all she said.

"Oh, go on, Rubes," Lily pleaded, scrambling out after Molly. "What is it? Don't leave us in suspense!"

Ruby laughed. Lily lived over the road from Molly and was loud, funny and dramatic. "I'll tell you once Kitten Club gets started, OK?" she promised, waving goodbye to her mum.

Ruby, Lily and Molly dashed up to Ella's front door and rang the bell. There were six members of Kitten Club altogether – the three of them, plus Ella, Mia and Amy. They had met back in the summer, when they'd each chosen a kitten from Chestnut Farm. The girls had got along so well, they'd decided to form a club so that they could keep in touch with each other – and the kittens too, of course! Every Saturday afternoon, the girls took it in turns to host a Kitten Club meeting at their house, and always had lots of fun.

"Hiya!" Ella said, opening the front door. She was holding her tabby and white kitten, Honey, who stared at them with big green eyes, then let out a squeaky meow as if to say hello too. "Oh, look, here comes Amy too. Hi, Amy!"

The girls turned to see blonde-haired Amy getting out of a car and hurrying up the path towards them. "Hi," she said, smiling at everyone.

Ruby, Lily, Molly and Amy went inside just as a boy with the same sandy hair as Ella sauntered downstairs. His eyebrows shot up as he saw them. "Whoa, girl invasion," he said, pretending to look scared. "Time to get

out of here." He leaped down the last few stairs, shoved his feet in some battered trainers, and headed for the front door. "I'm going round to Jake's, Mum," he called.

"Nice to see you too, Finn," said Ella, rolling her eyes. "This is Finn, my twin brother. Finn, this is Lily, Molly, Ru—"

But Finn was already out of the door. "Laters!" he shouted.

Ruby noticed that Amy, who was an only child, looked rather taken aback at Finn's rudeness. Molly, on the other hand, who had three brothers, grinned good-naturedly. "Boys," she said, shaking her head.

The doorbell rang again, and there was Mia on the doorstep. "Sorry I'm late," she said, seeing that everyone else had already arrived. "Aisha had a tantrum about having her shoes put on and it took ages to get out of the house." She reached over to stroke Honey, who had clambered up on to Ella's shoulder. "Hello, cutie!"

"How's Smokey?" Ruby asked Mia, as Ella led everyone through to the living room. "I hope he hasn't tried to escape again?"

Mia laughed. At the last Kitten Club meeting, she'd told the others how Smokey, her fluffy grey kitten, had got outside and had an unexpected adventure in the big wide world. The kittens weren't supposed to go out until they'd had their second set of vaccinations and Smokey hadn't been wearing a collar, so Mia had been worried sick. Thankfully, he had returned home safely before too long. "He's even more desperate to get out now that he's had a taste of freedom," she replied. "But I've

managed to keep all the doors shut."

"Not long to go, is it?" Ella said, as they sat down in the living room. She put Honey on the floor and the little kitten rushed over to bat a paw at the lace dangling from one of Molly's trainers. "Honey's got her next lot of vaccinations this week – and then she'll be able to go into the garden too. She can't wait. She hates seeing Misty go in and out, while she has to stay indoors."

Misty, who was curled up on the windowsill in the sunshine, was the other cat who lived with Ella's family. She was rather an old lady cat, and Ella had often told the girls how poor Misty got fed up with cheeky Honey pestering her to play.

Ella's mum came in with a tray of drinks, and a plate of cookies, grapes and plums. "Hello, girls," she said. "Nice to see you all again."

Everyone said hello and helped themselves to a drink.

"I think Ziggy will love being outside," Ruby said, biting into a juicy plum and smiling as she thought about her own adventurous kitten. "He's always got so much energy, I can just imagine him scampering all over the place – up trees, through the long grass, in and out of the neighbours' gardens…"

"Our vet said we have to leave it a week or so after their second vaccinations," Amy remembered. She gave a little smile. "Dad's put in a cat flap now, but Ginger still seems such a baby, I'm not sure he'll be strong enough to push the door open!"

"We've got a cat flap too," Molly said, "although we're keeping it locked until Truffle can go out. She's curious about it already – she keeps going up to it and tapping at it as if she knows it's her own special door."

Everyone laughed. Then Ella opened up the Kitten Club scrapbook and did the roll-call. Each girl had chosen a secret Kitten Club name and gave a little meow when Ella called it out. The meetings tended to start with the roll-call, then everyone shared their kitten news. Ruby was desperate to share her news, so as soon as the last name had been called, she made her announcement.

"I've got something really exciting to say!" she burst out. "And you'll never guess what it is!"

Chapter 2

Lily turned eagerly to look at Ruby. "Ah! Is this the mysterious You-Know-What?" she asked.

Ruby grinned. "It is," she said. "So here goes. I know we've only just had a meeting at my house, but Mum says, as it's my birthday next Saturday, would you all like to come for a Kitten Club *sleepover* at mine?"

She pulled a handful of pink envelopes from her skirt pocket. "Ta-da!"

"Oooh!" Molly squealed, as Ruby handed out the invitations. "What, *all* of us? That would be so cool!"

"A Kitten Club sleepover? Definitely!" Ella cried. "Count me in!"

"And me!" Mia added.

"Yes, please," Amy said, turning pink with excitement.

"Woo-hoo! What a brilliant idea!" Lily cheered. "It's a date!"

For the next ten minutes, the girls could talk of nothing other than the Kitten Club sleepover. "We'll have to have a midnight feast!" Ella said. "And play loads of games."

"We can tell ghost stories," giggled Lily. "Really spooky ones!"

"And talk about our kittens *all night*," Amy beamed.

"Check with your parents and let me know," said Ruby. "I really hope you can all come!" She grinned. "A Kitten Club sleepover will be the best birthday present ever!"

Later that week, each member of Kitten Club phoned Ruby to tell her the good news. They could all come to her birthday sleepover on Saturday! Ruby was thrilled. She'd had sleepovers with Molly before, but never with *five* friends at once! Every time she thought about it, she felt tingly.

"You'll enjoy it too, Ziggy," she told her
kitten, as he chased after his
favourite cat toy, a fluffy
snake on a string that
she was pulling around
the living room.

"What a lot of fuss
you'll get from
everyone! We might
even sneak you into my
room to join the sleepover;
would you like that?"

Ziggy did a huge leap and pounced on
the toy snake, his body quivering with
delight, and Ruby laughed. "I'll take that as
a yes," she said.

"Ruby! Max! Get your shoes on, it's
nearly time to go!"

Her mum's voice made Ruby jump, and her eyes jerked to the clock on the mantelpiece. Four o'clock already? Oh no. She wasn't looking forward to this. She put her shoes on, then scooped up Ziggy.

"Come on, sweetie," she said. "We've got to go to the vet's. Time for your next set of vaccinations, I'm afraid."

Ziggy purred happily as she stroked him, and Ruby felt even worse as she took him into the kitchen, where her mum had the cat-carrying box ready. She knew he wouldn't be purring once they got to the vet's.

"There we are," she said, putting him gently into the box. Mum had laid an old jumper inside it for Ziggy to snuggle up on, but he didn't seem to want to lie down. Instead he stood on his back legs and tried to scramble out again, and Ruby had to close the lid quickly to stop him.

"Sorry, Zig," she said, through an airhole in the lid. "This is the last lot of vaccinations for ages though. And in a week or so, you'll be able to go outside. It'll all be worth it, I promise."

Ruby had a heavy heart as she carried the box out to the car. Even though she knew the vaccinations were for the best, there was still something horrible about the thought of a sharp needle going into her kitten. Ziggy really hadn't been his usual bouncy self after his first vaccinations, and she wasn't looking forward to seeing him that way again.

Max was making a huge fuss about being strapped into his car seat, kicking and shouting. Ruby hung back, not wanting the noise to frighten Ziggy. "Don't want to go," he wailed crossly, drumming his heels. "Don't want to GO!"

"We'll be back before you know it," Mum said, snapping in the clasp. Then she helped Ruby with her seat belt. "Don't worry, honey," she said, giving Ruby a hug. "It'll be over in a flash."

Thankfully, Ruby's mum was right. For once the waiting room at the vet's was empty, and they were seen straight away. The vet was very kind and friendly, and Ruby barely had time to worry about Ziggy before the vaccination had been done. Even Max behaved himself, holding Mum's hand quietly while they were in there. Then, as they were on their way out, Mum noticed there were some pet items for sale on the reception desk.

"Look, there are some cat collars here. We should get one for Ziggy – do you want to choose?" she said to Ruby.

Ruby set Ziggy's box down on a chair, and examined the range of collars. There were all sorts of different colours and styles – some flea collars, some bright sparkly ones, some plain, and some with little bells hanging from them. "Want a Spider-Man one!" Max said, straining to see on his tiptoes.

"I'm afraid we don't have any," the lady on reception said with a laugh.

Ruby chose a blue sparkly collar with a silver bell that would jingle whenever Ziggy moved. "That way I'll be able to hear him around the house," she said, smiling.

"And the birds will hear him coming too, and can fly off before he tries to catch them," Mum added. "Good choice. We'll take this one, please," she said to the receptionist.

"Would you like an identity disc with that?" the lady asked, showing them a round silver tag. "We can get it engraved for Saturday if that's convenient."

"Yes, please," Mum said. She smiled at Ruby. "We'll put his name and our phone number on it, just in case he ever gets lost."

Ruby nodded. Knowing her crazy kitty, he *would* get lost – within five minutes of being let out, no doubt. He was a born adventure-cat!

Mum gave the lady their details for the disc, then paid for everything. The lady gave them the collar to take home and a receipt to show they'd paid for the tag too.

Ziggy didn't take too long to get over his vaccinations, thank goodness. He was off his food that evening, and, like last time, seemed rather grouchy and irritable, but by the following morning, he was absolutely fine again, bounding about all over the house as usual.

"That's great," Ruby said, cuddling him happily. "I'm glad you'll be fighting fit for the sleepover, Ziggy. Everyone's looking forward to it, especially me. It's going to be brilliant!"

Chapter 3

Once the vet visit was over, the rest of the
week got better and better. At home, Mum
and Dad kept whispering about secret
birthday things, and at school, Ruby made
lots of plans for the sleepover with Molly
and Amy. Then on Friday afternoon, Ruby
helped her mum with the party shopping,
and chose lots of yummy treats – crisps,

sausage rolls, cupcakes and chocolate fingers. "Can we have one *now*?" Max kept asking longingly as the trolley filled up.

When it came to Saturday, Ruby woke up with a big smile on her face. It was her birthday – and the day of the Kitten Club sleepover! Her parents came into her bedroom with a tray of breakfast things, and lots of presents.

"Open them, open them!" Max shouted, bouncing on Ruby's bed.

Ruby laughed as Ziggy burst through the door and scrambled on to her bed too. She should have known her kitten wouldn't want to miss out on any fun. Sure enough, as she started opening her presents, he was soon pouncing on the ribbon ends and fighting the wrapping paper like a mad thing!

Ruby received lots of lovely presents –
some new boots from Grandma, a pretty
bracelet from her Aunty Lucy, and a book
about cats from Max, but the best present
of all was downstairs. It was a bright pink
bike with a silver bell and ribbons
dangling from the handlebars.
"It's perfect!" she cried,
throwing her arms around her
mum and dad. "Thank you!"
After she'd got dressed and been out for
a ride on the new birthday bike, Ruby helped

her mum get everything ready for the
sleepover. There wasn't enough space to
have all six girls sleeping in Ruby's bedroom,
so they decided to set up the playroom as a
dormitory instead. There was a sofa bed in
there already, and Dad had borrowed some
camp beds from the neighbours.

"It'll be a bit of a squeeze but I think
we'll get you all in," Mum said with a laugh,
her arms full of pillows.

"It's great," said Ruby, making a grab
for Ziggy, who was dashing about madly.
She didn't want him to trip Mum up! The
playroom had a small TV, and Dad had
already said he'd rig up the DVD player
to it so they could watch a film later. And
Ruby had fetched the portable CD player
from her bedroom so that they could play

some party music. She grinned to herself.
She couldn't imagine there was going to be
all that much sleeping at the sleepover —
they'd be way too busy having fun!

While Ruby blew up balloons and decorated
the playroom with colourful streamers,
Mum nipped out to the vet's to pick up the
identity disc for Ziggy's collar. Ruby hadn't
wanted to put the collar on Ziggy straight
after his vaccinations in case it made him
feel even more grumpy, but now was the
perfect time to try it on. The identity disc
looked so smart with Ziggy's name
engraved on it!

"Here," Ruby said, scooping him up and
plopping him on her lap as she sat on the

kitchen floor. "I've got a present for you."
Ruby fastened the collar around his neck
before he could wriggle away. His neck was
still so small that she had to put the collar on
its tightest setting so that it wouldn't fall off,
but she took care not to pull it too tight.

"There," she said, once it was securely
fastened. "What do you think of that,
Ziggy?"

Ziggy didn't seem to like the new collar
at all! He squirmed irritably and tried to
kick it off with his back
leg. When that didn't
work, he shook his
head from side to
side, looking startled
when the little silver
bell tinkled!

Then he rushed across the room, ears back, as if he was trying to run away from the collar – but of course it came with him, the bell jingling the whole time.

Ruby couldn't help giggling. "Does it feel a bit strange?" she asked, watching as he lay on his side and tried to bite the collar. She went over and stroked him. "You'll get used to it, Ziggy. After all, you're going to have to wear it when you go out."

"The neighbourhood had better brace itself," Mum laughed, as Ziggy rolled over and over, biting and clawing at the collar. "There'll be a wildcat on the loose soon!"

After lunch, the Kitten Club girls arrived. Molly and Lily were first, each with a card

and a present for Ruby. Molly gave her a
necklace with a cat
pendant dangling from
it, and Lily's present
was some pretty hair
clips and a new set of
felt-tip pens. "Thank
you," Ruby cried, trying on
the necklace and putting in a hair clip.
"Come and see Ziggy. He's modelling *his*
new fashion accessory."

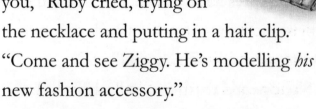

They went into the kitchen where
Ruby's mum was making drinks. Ziggy was
still rolling around on the floor, fighting
with his collar, and Molly let out a giggle.
"Truffle did exactly the same when we put
her collar on at first," she said. "She's used
to it now though."

The doorbell rang again just then. "That's probably more Kitten Clubbers," Ruby's mum said, setting glasses of squash on a tray. "Do you want to go and answer it, girls?"

Ruby, Molly and Lily all rushed to open the front door. There were Ella and Mia on the doorstep with their overnight bags … and more presents! "Come in, come in," Ruby smiled, hugging them each in turn. "Ooh, presents – thank you!"

She opened them excitedly. Ella had

given her a poster of a gorgeous tabby cat just like Ziggy, and Mia had wrapped up a set of silver bangles that clinked together when Ruby put them on.

"Thanks!" Ruby cried. "They're lovely."

The doorbell rang a third time, and they opened it to find Amy on the doorstep. "Happy birthday!" she said, smiling shyly. "I've been looking forward to this all week!" She handed Ruby another present, wrapped in shiny silver paper, tied with a bright pink bow.

Ruby unwrapped it eagerly to see a chunky silver photo frame. "I thought you could put a picture of Ziggy in it," Amy explained.

"I will – thank you," Ruby said, giving her a hug. "And now, who wants to see where we're all going to be sleeping tonight?"

"*Me!*" the girls shouted together.

Ruby led them through to the playroom

where the beds were all set out. "Ta-da!
What do you think?" she asked.

Lily grinned and dumped her overnight
bag on the nearest bed. "I think … pillow
fight!" she yelled, grabbing a pillow and
whacking Ruby over the head with it.

Giggling so hard she could barely
breathe, Ruby snatched up the nearest
pillow and biffed Lily back. Soon everyone

was fighting and screaming and falling over, helpless with laughter!

"Goodness me!" cried Ruby's mum, coming in after a few minutes. She was holding a tray of drinks and snacks, and looked amused to see all six girls squealing and scrapping, with pillows flying through the air. "I thought this was Kitten Club, not Wild Animal Club!"

Ruby sat up breathlessly from where she'd collapsed on the sofa bed and grinned. "Thanks, Mum. OK, everyone – time out! Let's have a drink, and get our club meeting started. There'll be plenty of time for pillow fighting later."

The girls sat on the sofa bed and drank thirstily. Then Ella produced the Kitten Club scrapbook and took out a pen. "Roll-call!" she declared. "Glamour-Puss?"

"Meow," said Ruby.

"Witch-Cat?" Ella asked.

"Meow," Mia answered.

"Moggy?" Ella said, but before Molly could reply, a tabby streak shot into the room and bounded up on to the sofa bed.

"Ziggy!" Amy cried in delight.

Meow, Ziggy answered, just as if he was

joining in the roll-call. Everyone giggled, and Ella solemnly wrote down his name and ticked it off on her register.

"Trust you, Ziggy," Ruby said, tickling him affectionately. "You're not shy, are you?"

Ziggy purred and blinked his green eyes as the girls all reached out to stroke him and make a fuss of him.

"Oh, look at that nice new collar," Mia said admiringly. "Aren't you smart?"

"I think he's going to enjoy today's Kitten Club just as much as us," Lily laughed. "Isn't that right, Ziggy?"

Chapter 4

The rest of the Kitten Club meeting was
brilliant. The girls wrote up their club news
in the scrapbook first, then Ruby's mum
brought out lots of coloured tissue paper,
some glue and a huge roll of lining paper.
The girls used the coloured paper to make a
big collage … of a kitten, of course! When
they'd finished, they left it to dry and went

out to play hide-and-seek in the garden, leaving Ziggy inside.

"Just think, this time next week, we'll be playing outside with our kittens," Mia said when they'd finished the game. "Won't that be cool?"

"The best," Ruby agreed. "Oh, look at Ziggy watching us through the window." She giggled at the sight of his eager little face, his furry ears pricked up into points. "He wishes he could come out here and join in, I bet."

"Teatime!" Ruby's mum called just then. "Come and wash your hands!"

The girls didn't need telling twice. Ruby's mum and dad had made a lovely party tea of sandwiches and sausage rolls, crisps, olives, chocolate fingers, grapes …

and best of all, a big birthday cake decorated with pink icing and scattered with silver sugar balls.

Everyone tucked in hungrily – especially Max – and later on, as Ruby blew out the candles on her cake and made a wish, she couldn't help feeling it was the most perfect birthday ever. She was already hoping that she could have a Kitten Club sleepover on her next birthday as well!

After tea, the girls put some music on in the playroom and had their very own birthday

disco. Ziggy got very excited and kept rushing in and out of the room, his bell jingling all the while as if he was joining in with the music.

Then Ruby's mum said it was time to change into their pyjamas and brush their teeth. After that, the six friends snuggled down in their sleeping bags, none of them feeling at all sleepy. They watched a funny DVD, then whispered ghost stories to each other in the darkness, giggling and squealing at the scary bits, before starting their midnight feast – well, a nine thirty feast anyway.

"Come on, girls, it's getting late," said Ruby's mum, putting her head round the door just then. "I think it's time to close your eyes and settle down to sleep now, OK?"

"OK, Mum," said Ruby, smiling in the darkness as Lily gave little pretend snores. "Good night, everyone."

"Good night," the others chorused.

As the girls got comfortable, silence fell across the room. It had been a busy, fun Kitten Club meeting and everyone was feeling quite tired.

Unfortunately, a certain tabby kitten was still wide awake! Mum had left the door slightly ajar and Ziggy sneaked in. He wandered over the girls' sleeping bags, playing with their hair and pouncing on their teddies.

"Ow!" giggled Ella, as the cheeky kitten pulled and chewed her long hair. "Stop that, Ziggy!"

"Oof!" squeaked Mia in surprise. "He's just jumped right on to my tummy!"

"Come here, you little monkey," Ruby said, reaching out and scooping him up. "Lie down quietly with me, there's a good boy."

Of course, Ziggy being Ziggy, he had no intention of being good or quiet, and promptly started a fight with the drawstring at the top of Ruby's sleeping bag. Ruby was just beginning to think she'd have to shut him in the kitchen for the rest of the night, when Ziggy suddenly gave a big yawn. Then he curled up on Ruby's pillow, tucked his tail neatly around himself and shut his eyes. Everyone was asleep within seconds.

The next morning, the girls slept in late and Ruby's dad made them all pancakes for breakfast. Everyone agreed it had been the best Kitten Club meeting *ever*!

"I think it's my turn for the next meeting," Lily said when her mum arrived, carrying Jessica, Lily's baby sister, to take Lily and Molly home. "So I'll see you all on Saturday at my house, OK? Thanks, Ruby. That was such fun." She leaned down to give Ziggy a last stroke. "See you soon, wildcat. Have fun in the great outdoors!"

"Oh, he will," Ruby said with a smile. "There's no doubt about that!"

On Tuesday, it had been a whole week since Ziggy's second set of vaccinations so he

was officially allowed outside. Ruby felt so
excited at the thought of taking him out
into the garden that she could hardly
concentrate at school, and couldn't wait
to get home.

Ziggy was asleep in his basket when she
arrived back, and she scooped him up and
kissed his little head. "Hello, lovely," she
said, snuggling him close to her. "Are you
ready for an adventure?" She laughed to
herself. "What am I saying? Of course you
are. You're *always* ready for an adventure!"

"I'll come with you," Mum said, "just in
case he makes a break for it, and we have to
catch him."

"Me too," Max said. "I run fast!"

Ruby opened the back door and carried
Ziggy outside, followed by Mum and Max.

It was October, but it was a warm and
sunny day – perfect for Ziggy's first time
exploring the garden. Ruby sat down on the
grass with him on her lap, expecting him to
leap off immediately and start charging
about in true Ziggy style. She held her
breath as she let go of him.

"And … he's off!" Mum joked.

But to their surprise, he *wasn't* off.
In fact, Ziggy stayed right where he was
on Ruby's lap, his tiny claws digging into
her school skirt.

"Go on then," Ruby said, unhooking his
claws and putting him gently on the lawn.
"You can explore, you know!"

Ziggy let out a nervous squeak and
scrambled straight back on to Ruby's lap.
Then he buried his head in her school

jumper, as if he didn't even want to *look* at the garden, let alone *be* in it!

"Oh, bless him," Mum said, crouching down and stroking him. "Fancy tearaway Ziggy being such a scaredy-cat!"

"It's OK, Zig," Ruby said encouragingly, and tried to put him down, but once again, he seemed to panic at the thought of being on the ground. He clung on to her, meowing plaintively, his eyes big and frightened.

"He doesn't like it," Max said, sounding disappointed.

Ruby felt disappointed too – and puzzled. This was not how she'd expected Ziggy's first outdoor adventure to go at all. "Well, I guess there's no point in making you stay out here if you don't like it," she said after a moment. "Let's go back inside. We can try again tomorrow."

But the same thing happened again on Wednesday when she tried to encourage Ziggy outside. And on Thursday, when Ziggy heard the back door open, he actually fled upstairs in alarm.

"Come on, Zigster," Ruby said, when she found him under her bed, his eyes wide and his tail all fluffed up. "There's no need to be scared. It's fun out there!"

"Let's try putting his food bowl just outside the back door," Ruby's mum suggested. "That might tempt him out."

Ruby thought that was a good idea. "Ziggy, teatime!" she called, rattling the box of kitten food. She carefully mashed some up with water in his food bowl, and sure enough, while she was doing that, she felt Ziggy's fluffy body winding around her legs. He was rumbling with purrs now and giving impatient little meows.

"Good boy." Ruby kept her voice soft.
"Here's your bowl," she said, carrying it
high up. Ziggy ran after her, gazing at it
hungrily. Then he stopped dead as Ruby
opened the back door and set the bowl
down outside. She crouched next to the
bowl, holding out her hand towards him
encouragingly. "Come on then! I know
you're hungry."

Ziggy hesitated. She could see his little nose sniffing the air. He could obviously smell the food, but didn't move any nearer the back door.

"Come on, Ziggy," Ruby coaxed again. "I'm here. There's nothing to worry about!"

But Ziggy backed away from the open door, his tail drooping. Then he turned and disappeared from the room. Clearly even food wasn't going to tempt him outside!

Ruby sat back on her heels, feeling rather stumped. Poor Ziggy! Why was he so scared? And how in the world could she make him realize that the garden was a fun place to be?

Chapter 5

"I just don't know what to do!" Ruby sighed. It was the following day at school, and she, Molly and Amy were out in the playground for morning break. "Ziggy's being such a wuss! He won't even *try* to go outside."

Molly's eyebrows shot up. "What – crazy Ziggy? The same animal that was tearing across our beds last Saturday,

trampling over our heads?" she asked.
"You're kidding, right?"

"Nope," Ruby replied. "He seems really
frightened whenever I try to take him out.
He trembles and clings to me as if he's
totally freaked out."

"Wow," Amy said in surprise. "That
doesn't sound like him."

"I know," Ruby said. "I thought I'd have trouble stopping him, but it's completely the opposite. Have your kittens been out?"

"Not yet," Molly said. "I might take Truffle out this afternoon as my brothers have got football practice, and the garden will be nice and quiet. How about you, Amy?"

"I'm going to try Ginger outside today too," Amy replied. "I had Drama Club last night so didn't get in until it was late. I didn't think it was a good idea to take Ginger on his first trip out in the dark!" She put a comforting hand on Ruby's arm. "Don't worry about Ziggy. He'll be fine."

"I hope so," said Ruby. "I'll try again after school. He probably just needs to get used to the big wide world after all these weeks staying indoors."

Unfortunately though, when Ruby took
Ziggy out that afternoon, he still showed
absolutely no sign of getting used to going
outside, or wanting to be there at all. Every
time she tried to put him on the ground, he
dug his claws in and clung to her, refusing
to let her detach him.

Ruby sighed, feeling wretched as she
brought him back inside. What could she
do to help him get over his fears? She was
glad it was going to be Kitten Club again
the next day. She hoped her friends might
have some bright ideas!

But when Ruby got to Lily's house on
Saturday, it seemed as if the other girls could
talk of nothing other than how much *their*

kittens were all loving the great outdoors.

"Honey is having a whale of a time —
but unfortunately Misty isn't!" Ella said,
leaning back on the big squashy sofa in
Lily's living room and letting out a sigh.
"Before, when Honey had to stay in, Misty
always liked to escape into the garden to get
some peace and quiet, but that's all changed
now. Honey follows her *everywhere*."

Mia chuckled, stroking Lily's black
kitten, Buster, who had curled up asleep on
her lap. "Smokey thinks it's Christmas every
day now he can go out. He runs round like
a loon, sniffing everything and trying to get
next door any chance he can…" She rolled
her eyes. "We've put an identity tag on his
collar just in case he goes adventuring too
far again."

"Ginger was a bit scared about going outside at first," Amy said. "Every time the wind blew his fur or he heard a noise from one of the other gardens, he almost jumped out of his skin. I took him out again this morning though, and he loved it. I haven't let him go out for very long, just half an hour or so. The vet told us to build up the time gradually until he's used to it."

"That's what we're doing too," Molly said. "Truffle's having such fun. She likes pouncing on the grass whenever it moves. She even climbed halfway up the cherry tree yesterday – then got stuck!"

"Buster likes rolling around on the path when it's sunny," Lily said. "His fur gets all warm and dusty. I must take a photo of him to go in our scrapbook." She turned to Ruby. "How about Ziggy? I bet he's a maniac outside, isn't he?"

Ruby sighed and shook her head. "Not at all – he won't even *go* outside," she admitted. "I've tried everything to tempt him out, but he just doesn't want to leave the house. He's scared stiff. I don't know what to do!" She turned to Amy. "Amy, you said Ginger was a bit nervous at first. What made him more confident about going out?"

"I took some of his favourite toys into the garden," Amy replied. "He's got a jingly ball that he loves chasing. I rolled it out of

the back door and he ran straight after it.
It took him a few moments to realize he
was outside, I think, and then he was fine.
Too busy chasing after his ball to worry
about anything else!"

"That sounds a good idea," Ruby said,
brightening. "I'll try that with Ziggy.
He's got a fluffy snake he likes chasing.
Hopefully seeing it outside will make
him want to follow it."

After the girls had written up their
Kitten Club news in the scrapbook, Lily's
mum appeared. "I've just got Jessica off
to sleep, so do you fancy making some
pom-pom kittens?" she asked. "I've got
pom-poms, googly eyes, ears, tails …
even whiskers!"

"Yes, please!" the girls chorused.

They went into the kitchen and sat around the table, glueing eyes, ears and whiskers to the pom-pom heads, and pipe-cleaner tails to the pom-pom 'bodies'. "These are the wonkiest whiskers ever," Molly giggled as she attached hers.

"Well, my kitten looks cross-eyed," Ella spluttered, holding her pom-pom head up to show the others. "Poor thing!"

Buster, meanwhile, was having a lovely time chasing a stray pom-pom around on the floor beneath their feet. He wound in and out of the chair legs like a black fluffy streak.

Later on, while the pom-pom kittens were drying, the girls took Buster into the garden for a quick play. Lily was putting his litter tray out now, to encourage Buster to start going to the toilet outside. "I can't wait until he stops using the litter tray all together," she sighed. "Cleaning it out is definitely my worst job. It smells even worse than Jessica's nappies!"

Ruby loved watching Buster exploring the garden. He seemed to find it so much fun, prancing through the grass, stopping to sniff at leaves and pebbles, then making a dive for a dandelion that was swaying in the wind.

"Ooh, Buster's being very brave today," Lily said, as the little black kitten scampered right to the end of the garden. "He's never ventured so far from the house before. Good boy." She grinned. "It must be because you lot are here, and he knows you'll report back to his brothers and sisters!"

Ruby felt a pang of envy as Buster trotted about so happily, rushing from girl to girl, his fluffy tail up in the air. She couldn't wait to see Ziggy like this in her garden. How she hoped Amy's suggestion would work, and Ziggy would want to explore soon!

Chapter 6

Back at home later that afternoon, Ruby wasted no time in getting out Ziggy's favourite fluffy snake toy. It had started off a creamy-white colour, but it was rapidly getting grubbier and grubbier, as it had been dragged around the floor by Ziggy and chewed and mauled.

Ziggy had been dozing in an armchair,

but his ears pricked up when he heard
Ruby's voice. "Ziggy! Look what I've got!"

His eyes opened sleepily, and then he
noticed the fluffy snake being pulled along
the carpet – and instantly he was wide
awake. He got to his feet, shook himself,
then leaped off the chair in pursuit of
the snake, galloping along after Ruby as
she ran in front of him. "Come and get it!"
Ruby teased, pulling it around the kitchen
chair legs.

Ziggy bounded after the snake, his ears
back with excitement and his eyes round
and shining.

"Can't catch me," Ruby called, dangling
it high in the air, so that Ziggy jumped up
athletically after it, trying to grab it with his
little claws.

Ruby led him all the way back into the living room, then let him have it and fight it for a moment. She returned to the kitchen and opened the back door just a crack, then went to find Ziggy again and untangled the snake from his paws. He rushed playfully after her as she dragged the snake along the ground, heading back into the kitchen.

Ziggy chased the snake all the way across the room and right up to the back door, almost slipping on the tiled floor with his eagerness to get it. Feeling excited herself now – was Amy's trick going to work? – Ruby slipped through the back door, pulling the fluffy snake temptingly after her.

She held her breath as she waited, hoping that Ziggy would charge out too…

but nothing happened. She threw the end
of the snake back through the door and
tugged it so that just the tip was left in the
kitchen. "Come on, Ziggy," she called.
"Catch it if you can!"

After a few seconds, a
small furry face peeped
tentatively round the
edge of the door.
Ziggy's eyes were wide
and his fur was fluffed
up all over.

Ruby dropped to her
knees and held out her hand.
"Come on," she coaxed. "Come and play."
And she tugged the string attached to
the snake so that it plopped down on to
the garden path.

Ziggy looked at the snake, then at Ruby, then at the garden. But instead of leaping out to carry on playing, he vanished inside.

Ruby sighed in frustration. Ziggy was proving very stubborn when it came to exploring the garden! How would she ever get him to be brave and come outside?

The next day was Sunday, and Ruby's family were going to her grandma's house for lunch. Aunty Jane, Mum's sister, was going to be there with her new baby Freddie, and Mum had sorted out a big plastic bag of baby clothes to give her, which she'd left by the radiator in the hall. "Into the car, kids," she shouted, while Ruby's dad locked the back door. "Come on, Ruby, hurry up, love."

"I just want to say goodbye to Ziggy,"
Ruby replied, dashing towards the stairs.
Ziggy hadn't been in the kitchen when she'd
looked, so he was probably up in her
bedroom, she thought.

"There's no time for that now," said
Mum, heaving up the bag by its handles.
"Come on, get into the car."

She stowed the bag of clothes in the
boot and settled Max into his car seat. Ruby
climbed in beside him – she was sad not to
have said goodbye to Ziggy, but they
weren't going to be gone for long. Dad put
some music on, and Ruby sang along. Once
or twice she thought she'd heard a strange
high-pitched squeaking sound, but then she
realized Max was playing with one of his
toy trucks. It was probably a squeaky wheel

on the truck, she decided.

After about half an hour, they arrived at Grandma's house. "Hello, Ruby, hello, Max!" Grandma cried, hurrying out of the house to greet them. "Come on in."

Mum had opened the boot to take out the bag of clothes – and suddenly clapped a hand to her mouth. "Oh! Ruby, I think you should take a look at this first," she said. "Guess who's come along for the ride?"

Ruby ran to see what her mum was talking about – had one of her dolls fallen into the bag or something? She gasped as she looked into the car. It wasn't a *doll* that was in the bag of clothes but…

"Ziggy!" she exclaimed in disbelief. "What are you doing in there?"

There inside the bag of clothes, cuddled

up on a velvety babygro, was Ziggy!

"Those little squeaks I heard on the journey – it must have been him meowing!" Ruby realized, reaching down to pick up her travelling kitten. "Ziggy Jackson! For a kitten who's too scared to go outside, you've come a long, long way today!"

Chapter 7

Grandma bustled over to see what was happening and laughed out loud at the sight of the stowaway. "My goodness! So this is Ziggy, is it? Well, you'd better all come in." She smiled. "Bella's going to get a surprise – it's not often *she* gets a visitor."

Ruby smiled too. Bella was Grandma's old fluffy grey cat. "Come on, Ziggy," she

said, cuddling him close. "You are a funny
thing. I bet you had a surprise, didn't you,
when your comfortable bed suddenly began
moving!"

Grandma took them inside to her warm,
sunny kitchen, where Bella was curled up in
her cosy basket near the radiator. Ruby
wasn't sure how Ziggy would react to
another cat and put him down on the floor
rather cautiously, half expecting him to try
to scramble back into her arms. To her
surprise though, he gave a pleased-
sounding meow at the sight of
Bella, trotted right over
to her and snuggled
against her side, as if
he thought she was
his mummy!

"How sweet." Grandma chuckled. "Let's hope Bella doesn't mind. Sometimes cats aren't very friendly with other cats."

Luckily, Bella seemed quite happy to find Ziggy cuddling up to her. She licked his fur, just as if she was his real mummy, and moved over a little to make more room for him in the basket.

"She likes him!" cried Max in delight.

"Ahhh," Ruby cooed, thrilled to see her kitten with Grandma's cat. "Good old Bella. Don't they look cute together?"

"Very cute," agreed Ruby's dad. Bella was washing Ziggy all over now, and they were both purring like old friends. Then the two cats settled down to sleep together, their purrs gently dying away as they dozed off.

The doorbell rang, and Grandma went

to answer it. It was Aunty Jane with baby Freddie, and everyone made a big fuss of them. Then Ruby and Max played with some Lego together while Grandma started making lunch. After a while Ruby noticed Bella getting up and stretching, opening her mouth in a long yawn. Then she stepped out of the basket, taking care not to disturb Ziggy, and padded across the floor towards the back door.

Perhaps it felt colder in the basket without big, fluffy Bella next to him, because Ziggy woke up a moment later. He looked all around him, as if wondering where his new mummy had gone. Then his eyes widened as he caught sight of her heading away from him. Ziggy immediately scrambled out of the basket and trotted after her.

Ruby smiled as she watched him. Ziggy was certainly very taken with Grandma's cat! Then she stiffened as she realized that Bella was approaching her cat flap. Uh-oh. She hoped Ziggy wouldn't be too disappointed when his new best friend disappeared.

Bella clambered rather inelegantly through the cat flap and it swung shut behind her. The door of the cat flap

was made of clear plastic, and Ziggy
scampered up to it and stared through.

Ruby crouched down next to him and
they watched Bella together. "Are you sure
you don't want to go out there with her?"
she asked Ziggy, stroking him. "Grandma,
can I open this door for Ziggy, to see if he
wants to go out?"

Grandma looked rather doubtful. "I'm
not sure. We don't want him running away,
or getting lost here, do we?" she said.

Ruby wrinkled her nose. "I don't think
that's something we need to worry about,"
she replied, and explained to Grandma the
problems she'd had getting Ziggy to
venture out at all.

Grandma nodded understandingly.
"I see," she said. "Well, let's find out if

my Bella can encourage him to be brave, shall we?"

She opened the door and Ruby went outside, knowing that Ziggy was watching her. She made a big show of going up to Bella, who was sitting on a sunny patch of the lawn, and stroking her. "Come on, Ziggy, you come out too," she urged.

Ziggy hesitated on the doorstep, watching Ruby and Bella there in the garden.

Ruby held her breath. Would Ziggy actually have the courage to come outside on his own?

Bella noticed Ziggy and meowed to him. Then, as he continued to stand in the doorway, the older cat got up and walked slowly over to him. Ruby and Grandma watched as kind Bella licked Ziggy's face

and then went a little way back into the
garden. She turned and looked at Ziggy, her
head on one side, and meowed again. Ruby
smiled. It was just as if Bella was saying,
"Well, hurry up then. What are you waiting
for?" to scaredy-cat Ziggy.

"Come on," Ruby called. She went over
and scooped him up, then sat on the grass
next to Bella with him on her lap. Ziggy felt
tense and rigid in her hands, but Bella gave
him another lick, and Ziggy's little furry
body relaxed and he began to purr.

Bella meowed and padded off towards the flowerbed. And all of a sudden, Ziggy got down from Ruby's lap … and trotted after her!

He went slowly and cautiously at first, his body low and flattened as if he was nervous. Suddenly, a bird squawked overhead and he jumped, startled, and stared up into the branches of a nearby tree. He then glanced at Bella, to see if this was something she was worried about too.

Bella had heard the bird as well and hissed up at it. Seeing this, Ziggy promptly tried his best to make a hissing noise at the bird too!

Ruby spluttered back a laugh, not wanting to offend her kitten.

At that moment, the wind blew, rustling the grass, which tickled Ziggy's tummy. He looked down at it in surprise, then dabbed a paw cautiously at some waving green blades. Then his ears shot back and he crouched low, wiggled his bottom and dived at a late-flowering daisy that was swaying in the breeze.

"That's it, Ziggy!" Ruby called out encouragingly. She couldn't stop smiling. Thanks to Bella, Ziggy had gained some confidence, and he seemed to be thoroughly enjoying himself. At last!

Chapter 8

"Tomboy?"

"Meow!"

"Glamour-Puss?"

"Meow!"

"And finally, me, Green-Eyes," Amy said with a smile. "Meow!"

It was the following Saturday, and Ruby and her friends were round at Amy's house

for another Kitten Club meeting. They were up in Amy's bedroom, taking it in turns to play with Ginger, Amy's gorgeous marmalade-coloured kitten, who was scampering about, very excited to have so many girls cooing over him!

This time, when it came to sharing their news, Ruby was able to report, with a big smile on her face, that Ziggy had got over his fear of the outside world, and loved playing in the garden.

"It was so cute the first time he braved it and went out after Bella," she told the others. "It was as if Bella was his mummy, looking after him and encouraging him."

"Good old Bella," Molly said. "I guess he felt like us, on our first day at school. I remember I wanted my mum with me!"

"I still can't believe Ziggy actually went in your car to your grandma's house," Mia giggled. "And I thought *Smokey* was an adventurous cat!"

"I'm glad Ziggy has discovered how much fun it is to explore the outside world on foot, as well as by car." Amy smiled.

"Yes, he loves it," Ruby said. "I was a bit worried that he wouldn't want to go out in our garden without Bella, but he was fine. In fact, the only problem I've got now, is keeping him in some of the time. He would be out all day long if I let him!"

After everyone had written up their news in the club scrapbook and stuck in some photos of their kittens playing outdoors, Amy's mum helped them bake some cookies together. "I've bought some icing pens, so when they've cooled down, you can decorate them." She smiled, as the girls took it in turns to stir the mixture.

"Cool!" said Lily. "We can ice kitten faces on to the cookies!"

"You can!" Amy's mum laughed. "And once we get that dough rolled out, we could

even cut it into kitten shapes."

When the chocolate chips had been
mixed in, the girls split the dough into six
piles and took turns to use the
rolling pin. With Amy's
mum's help, they cut
their cookie dough
into different shapes
– cat faces, of course,
or their initials. Then,
once they'd cleared
everything away and
Amy's mum had put the
cookies in the oven, the six
friends put on their jackets and took
Ginger out into the garden.

As Ginger rushed about chasing a small
ball and practised climbing the silver birch

tree, Ruby felt very happy knowing that
Ziggy enjoyed doing all those things too.

"It seems like ages since we first got our
kittens," Ella said, watching Ginger sprint
across the flowerbed. "Can you remember
what tiny babies they were? And look at
Ginger now – out and about like a really
grown-up cat!"

The six friends all gazed at Ginger –
then burst out laughing as he tried to
clamber up the fence and fell backwards
into a large flowering bush. "Oh, Ginger,"
Amy giggled, running to rescue him. She
picked him up and smiled at the others.
"The kittens may be growing up, but they're
just as funny as ever," she said.

"Too right," Ruby agreed, chuckling as
Ginger made a flying leap from Amy's arms,

then trotted off to explore another part of
the garden. Ruby smiled to herself, thinking
about all the lovely adventures she and
Ziggy were going to have together inside
and outside. Having a kitten was the best
fun ever!

Have you read...